The
Man~in~the~Moon
In Love

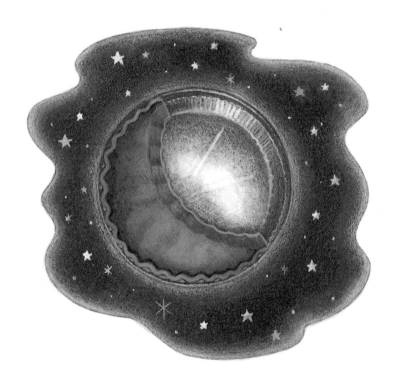

STORY BY
Jeff Brumbeau

ILLUSTRATIONS BY
Greg Couch

Stewart, Tabori & Chang

New York

For my mother, Dorothy
J. B.

To the memory of Eugene Sheppard, who gave his love of literature
to his daughter, my wife, Robin
G. C.

Text copyright © 1992 Jeff Brumbeau
Illustrations copyright © 1992 Greg Couch
Design by Paul Zakris

Published in 1992 by
Stewart, Tabori & Chang, Inc.
575 Broadway, New York, New York 10012

Library of Congress Cataloging-in-Publication Data
Brumbeau, Jeff.
    The man-in-the-moon in love / by Jeff Brumbeau ; illustrated by
Greg Couch.
        p.   cm.
    Summary: Some nights the Man-in-the-Moon is visible and some
nights he is not because of a bargain with the Man-in-the-Sun, permitting
one monthly visit between the Man-in-the-Moon and his lady love.
    ISBN 1-55670-229-9
    [1. Moon—Fiction.]   I. Couch, Greg, ill.   II. Title.
PZ7.B82837Man   1992
[E]—dc20   91-37804
                                                          CIP
                                                          AC

Distributed in the U.S. by Workman Publishing,
708 Broadway, New York, New York 10003
Distributed in Canada by Canadian Manda Group,
P.O. Box 920 Station U, Toronto, Ontario M8Z 5P9
Distributed in all other territories by
Little, Brown and Company, International Division,
34 Beacon Street, Boston, Massachusetts 02108

Printed and bound by Tien Wah Press (Pte), Ltd., Singapore
10 9 8 7 6 5 4 3 2 1

The
Man~in~the~Moon
In Love

*To Peg Johnston,
I'm glad you like my book!
Greg [signature]*

This is a story about the Man-in-the-Moon and why on some nights you can see him and why on other nights you cannot. Once he was always there, tending the light that made the moon shine every night of the year.

That was before something marvelous happened, and something sad, and something that in the end made him glad. The tale is still told on all the stars and planets, but it's one that begins a long time ago.

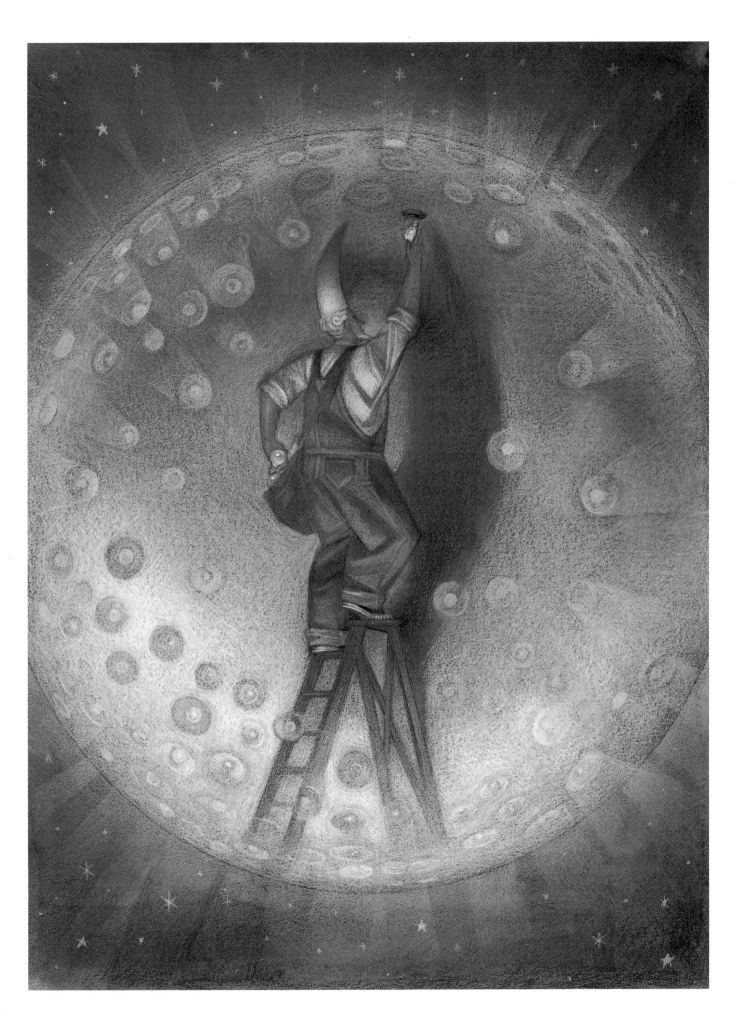

There was a woman who lived in a little blue house, deep in a forest glade. Not a town or city was near. She spent all of her days tending her garden and baking the sweet potato pies she made so well.

For many years she was happy. She could hear the whoosh of the wind in the pine trees and could see the forest hills outside her window. There was the tapping of rain on her slate roof to lull her to sleep, and the cooing of doves to wake her in the morning.

The woman had many good things, but she did not have a friend. At first it seemed to be no great matter. Then, as the years passed, she grew lonelier and lonelier, and more and more she wished she might find a friend.

One night while the woman was weeping from loneliness, a light came and peeked through her window. She looked out and up high in the black sky, and there she saw the Man-in-the-Moon. He seemed to be such a kind sort, that she thought she might tell him her woes.

So the woman climbed up to her rooftop, perched on top of the chimney, and emptied her heart.

Sailing slowly across the sky, the Man-in-the-Moon was busy with the business of the moon. But when he heard her sad words float up from earth, he stopped and looked down at the lonely woman. Then he put on his glasses, the better to hear her, and listened to her tale.

Now the Man-in-the-Moon also lived in a house by
himself and had done so for at least 999,991 years.
Almost no one came to visit him and, like the woman,
he too wished for a friend.

As soon as the woman was finished with her story, she
began to cry again.

"Don't cry," said the Man-in-the-Moon. "I would be
glad to be your friend."

The woman was so surprised to find that the moon could talk that she forgot all about her woes. But her story had so saddened the Man-in-the-Moon that now he began to cry.

One by one his tears raced by stars and clouds to splatter about the blue house. The woman had to dash inside to get her umbrella.

She was happy to have found a friend, even if he did live rather far away.

Every night thereafter, the woman climbed onto her roof to talk to the Man-in-the-Moon. After a while, she brought up an old armchair and table so she could sip her tea in comfort while they chatted.

It was not long before they fell in love and were married.

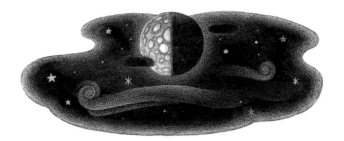

But they soon found that each had forgotten something very important. Because the woman could not fly up to live on the moon, the Man-in-the-Moon would have to come down to earth. First, however, he had to ask permission of the Man-in-the-Sun, who was in charge of all the planets, stars, and moons.

Now the Man-in-the-Sun was a fat, grouchy old grump who loved to do nothing but eat. And when he heard what the Man-in-the-Moon wanted, he was furious.

"Never!" he roared. "You are the Man-in-the-Moon and so in the moon you will stay! Now leave me alone while I eat my cake!"

This made the Man-in-the-Moon very sad. But the woman cheered him right up.

"I just know that one day you will come and live with me. And when you do, I'll have a fresh sweet potato pie waiting."

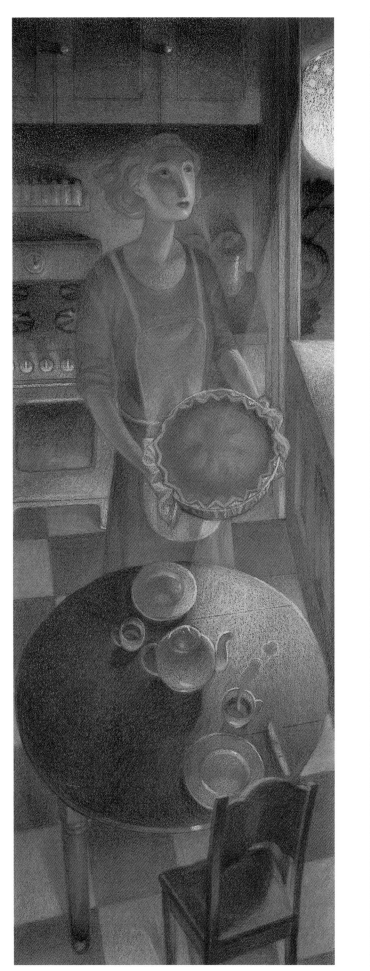

Many months went by and still they lived apart. Nevertheless, the woman was true to her word and every morning she baked a fresh sweet potato pie. And every night when her husband did not come, she ate it.

One day she said, "I must stop this. I'm becoming so fat that one morning I'll plop down in the bathtub and never get out again!"

So as not to waste the pies, however, she tied each one to a balloon and sent them drifting off into the sky. She hoped that this way some poor, hungry creature might find one.

The pies floated all over the world. A giraffe in Africa had one for lunch. A shark swimming in the ocean gulped another.

And one went high in the sky where the Man-in-the-Sun reached out a fiery hand and snatched it.

It tasted so good that he ordered the woman to make him fifty more pies immediately. But she was both wise and brave.

"You've only been mean to me and the Man-in-the-Moon. Why should I give something as nice as fifty sweet potato pies to someone as nasty as you?"

"Because if you do not," growled the Man-in-the-Sun, "I will burn you and your little blue house to the ground!"

"Go ahead," the woman said. "And then you will never taste another of my sweet potato pies."

The Man-in-the-Sun sizzled with rage. "All right," he grumbled. "What do you want?"

"For part of each month, my husband will live on earth with me. The other part of the month, he will stay in the moon and tend to the light. In return, you will receive one pie per week."

Flames flew out of the Man-in-the-Sun's eyes. Sparks whizzed and whistled down at the woman. But the Man-in-the-Sun's greed was so great that he had to agree.

The Man-in-the-Moon was full of joy. Quick as he could he went about turning out the lights of the moon. First one quarter went dark, then half, and then only a sliver of light was left. Finally the moon disappeared. At last the Man-in-the-Moon packed his bags and floated down to earth to live with the woman.

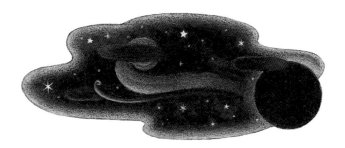

So if some night soon you look up in the sky and don't see the Man-in-the-Moon, you will know where he is. He is with his wife in a little blue house deep in a forest glade. They are eating sweet potato pie and they are very, very happy indeed.

The End